MW01248267

About the Author

She is thirty-seven-year-old woman. She lives in Texas and she has been writing short stories since grade school. This is her first publication. She enjoys reading scary stories in the rain and she loves nature.

The Prisoner

Laura Thibeault

The Prisoner

Olympia Publishers
London

www.olympiapublishers.com
OLYMPIA PAPERBACK EDITION

A CIP catalogue record for this title is
available from the British Library.

ISBN: 978-1-80439-337-6

This is a work of fiction.
Names, characters, places and incidents originate from the writer's
imagination. Any resemblance to actual persons, living or dead, is
purely coincidental.

First Published in 2024

Olympia Publishers
Tallis House
2 Tallis Street
London
EC4Y 0AB

Printed in Great Britain

Dedication

I dedicate this book to my family and friends for their support and encouragement throughout the years.

Acknowledgements

To my siblings Edward, Daniel & Judy for their encouragement. To my brother-in-law Ernesto, and sister-in-law Beatrice for their support. And to Christopher for just being the light in life. You inspire me more than you will ever know.

My life has never been easy. It is the reason that I am here. Some people believe that karma will catch up to you, while others believe that the path you walk will lead you straight to hell. Some even claim that if you seek blood, you will eventually meet up with the devil himself. I always believed that you make your own destiny that the devil or God does not exist. Yet, others will contradict me. I didn't believe in anything like that. Religion isn't my thing and I didn't care much for it. But that all changed the moment when he was brought into my cell block. Destiny had a way to intertwine our paths. Here is my story.

The night started off with the usual drama that a prisoner expects. Once you're incarcerated, you get used to seeing the dark side of humanity. We become animalistic in nature. Our survival instincts come through. And, rationalization does not exist. There were two guys beating up a prisoner as their initiation into the gang. When all of a sudden, we heard the guards bringing someone into our cell block. I quickly peered through the bars in hopes to see this new prisoner and thought he would most likely not last in this cell block. For you see this cell block where I resided, was known to store the most violent and aggressive inmates within the prison. The last few prisoners that were housed in this unit had been wasted in less than a week. Everyone began looking as the mysterious individual made his way down to his cell. He was seven feet tall and had long straight hair, and was covered in tattoos. He had a long bushy beard. I couldn't give you a description of his face though because it was covered with a burlap sack. Both hands and feet were shackled. I stood in awe as they walked him down to his cell and closed the cell door behind them.

I heard other prisoners scream obscenities at him, while others provoked him with sexual references. I however, found it alluring and mysterious. I wanted to know what his wrapsheet was. Why was he in here? I questioned. As I saw the guard walk pass my cell, I reached over and tugged at his sleeve. "Louie," I said. He turned around and stopped in front of my cell.

"What do you want, Silas?" he replied.

"Look, Louie, I just want to know what is up with that guy you just brought in?" I asked curiously.

Louie looked at me and rolled his eyes and said, "I wish I knew."

I looked at him puzzled and replied to his answer, "What the hell do you mean, you don't know." Of course I didn't believe his response; I knew that he knows what was going on or who this prisoner was, but he just didn't wish to disclose and it upset me to a whole new level. After a few moments of utter silence, he told me he was leaving and that he wished he could tell me. But how could he give information on someone he himself didn't know anything about. He told me that, in the meantime, I should stay away from that individual. I nodded and he took off.

I felt disheartened by Louie's response. I laid down in my bunk and just thought about how my life was different before I came to this place. Of course, as you may have assumed, I did have a family—a beautiful family. But life changes in an instant; I was married to my high school sweetheart. Her name was Camila. She had the most beautiful honey brown eyes you could ever imagine. Her smile radiated life. Her hair was as dark as the night sky, and she had the most infectious laugh you could possibly hear. She was the most loving, caring, and nurturing person I had ever met. Those were the attributes that made me fall in love with her. We had the perfect life. I worked as an executive accountant for a corporation. The money was great and it gave us stability. After a year into our marriage, Camila gave birth to twin boys. Their names were Jordan and Elliot. Those boys were the light of my life. They were my motivation in this world to become a better man. Everything I did was for them. I existed for them; they were practically the essence of my being and so was Camila.

One night, it all came crashing down on me. I was working late as I always did. When two unknown assailants broke into my home and slaughtered my family. No one truly knows the pain that is to have your whole life taken from you in an instant. Coming home to that horrendous scene was so traumatizing to me. There was cops everywhere; the sirens of ambulances screeching down the street. News media sweeping down the street, trying to get their input as to what happened and of course make their own assumptions. It's what they do. For years I struggled with depression and suicidal thoughts. I hated everything, this world had to offer. I felt I had been robbed of my happiness. I was hellbent on giving my family the retribution they so justly deserved. The police figured it was a home invasion and immediately closed the case. I felt as if there was more to this than just a home invasion. I thought to myself even if it truly is just two small-time burglars; I will be heartless and cold, show them no mercy as they did not show my family any clemency. I began asking around to check any video cameras from my neighborhood which neighbors were quick to oblige. The case was cold for a few years until word got back to me that two men down at Ronald O'Keeffe's bar were bragging about how they had murdered an entire family and gotten away with it.

Later that night, I asked Joseph McDaniel if by chance they were still down at the bar. He told me that when he heard this, he immediately came to tell me. But, if they weren't there anymore, most likely the manager Mateo O'Keeffe which was the owner's son, would know. I smiled and thanked him for the information. He hugged me and said, "I hope this revenge that you've got going on gives you peace son." Mr. McDaniel was a mature man. Had served in World War two. He was more of a mentor to me. I look up to that man in so many ways. He fought for our country and saw a lot of shit but he still managed to get back on his feet than let his demons defeat him.

I headed to O'Keeffe's and glanced at everyone at the bar. No one stood out to me, but I knew they had been there, and the anger grew in my heart. "What can I get you Silas?" Mateo asked.

"A double shot of whiskey please," I replied. Sitting down next to me, was a man, smoking a big Cuban cigar. The man was in his thirties, around my age. But he looked more rugged than I did. He had a flannel shirt, dirty stone washed ripped jeans, mountain climbing boots and a white ball cap that was perched on his shoulder length, black hair which he had pulled back in a ponytail. He looked at me coldly like my presence disturbed him. I turned around, tucked my hair behind my ears and said, "How are you?" He grunted and looked at me, took a puff of his cigar and blew it in my face. Mateo set the drink in front of me, and I took it, told him "Cheers" and gulped it down, never once breaking my gaze. The man sneered at me, got up and left. "What the hell was his problem?" I asked Mateo who was rearranging the bottles.

"He comes here regularly. He claims he drowns out his demons with alcohol and smoking," Mateo said.

"Demons," I said puzzled.

"Yeah, he's a war hero much like Mr. McDaniel," he replied.

"I see, war hangs so heavy on the soul," I told him.

"Why are you here?" Mateo asked. Now counting the till for the night.

"They told me about these two individuals that were here earlier on, they said they bragged about murdering a family, and well that's why I'm here. I wanted to see if I ran into them, but I think I missed them," I told Mateo.

Mateo looked at me and said, "Why are you doing this to yourself? It won't bring them back." I looked at him and gave him a cold look and left but I still had to fulfill an obligation to myself. I couldn't picture my life without them. Those two bastards had taken everything from me. My peace was gone for; I feared they would do this to others as well. I told myself that I wouldn't let that happen.

"Did you find them, my boy?" McDaniel asked. I shook my head in dismay. "Give it time, I'm sure they'll turn up." He gave me a cold long neck bottle of beer. I took it and we sat on the porch swing just talking about our troubles, and how life is nothing but a painful reminder of how the ones we've lost walk beside us every day. We stayed talking until the sun started coming up over the horizon. I was so wasted that I stumbled into my house once Mr. McDaniel and I said our goodbyes. I walked through my door and crashed out on the couch.

I was drifting to sleep when I was awoken by a hard knock on my door. I opened it and to my surprise my coworker Jennifer was standing on the other side of the door. "Hey," she said.

I looked at her and said, "What's up?" She looked at me and told me that I looked like shit. That she had just dropped by to check up on me. I smirked and thanked her for stopping by but that I was fine. She asked to come in because she showed me, she had brought breakfast and coffee. At first, I hesitated but then decided to let her in. We chatted for a few hours and it took my mind off of my agenda for a bit. But after she had left, my vengeful rampage came back again. It was so hard to control my vengeance. All I thought about was getting revenge, the sole revenge that I had been denied.

I bet you're wondering why I am here locked up in this prison. Well, I will have you know that I finally tracked down the two bastards that killed my family. According to rumors in the town they were two small-time burglars, just trying to make ends meet. People gossiped around town saying that they were two friends that had been down on their luck and had lost their jobs. But I for one didn't care. My ambition was greater than ever. So that night while they were standing outside O'Keeffe's bar, I confronted them. They basically confessed everything to me and I just lost control. My rage got the best of me. I shot them both in the head. Mateo at this time, witnessed everything and called the cops. "Don't you fucking move Silas!" he yelled. When the police came, they asked Mateo what happened. Mateo told him everything he had witnessed and that I had pulled the trigger.

One of the officers came over and tried to get my side of the story. But I told him that I had shot them in cold blood as retribution for taking my family. I told them since the law couldn't provide me closure; I gave myself private justice. I told them that it was an entitlement I felt that I so rightly deserved. The officers looked at each other, handcuffed me and put me in the back of the patrol car. Now, you may be wondering as to why Mateo called the cops on me in the first place. Why was he so reluctant to give me any information on these two scumbags? Well, I found out later they were very good friends of Mateo. When I took them out, he felt compelled to do his friends justice. Well at least in Mateo's eyes. Which in a way he did because I am here for life. But of course I didn't care if my life was pretty much over. I had accomplished what I had set out to do and I was proud of it.

Well, that's enough of my vengeance now let's get back to that day in the yard.

Later that day, they took us out to the yard. I walked around for a bit and noticed that the prisoner they had brought in was nowhere to be seen. "Hmmm," I thought to myself. I scouted around looking closely. Maybe I had missed him, but I couldn't see him. So, I sat down and contemplated my thoughts on how odd he looked. "Why was he wearing a burlap sack? Perhaps disfigurement of some kind," I said to myself.

"Hey, Silas, you got a cigarette?" Carlos, one of the fellow inmates asked.

I smirked and said, "Sure thing."

Carlos smiled and said, "Great. I've been dying for one

of these, nicotine will kill you."

I smiled and said, "Yes, I agree if this place doesn't do it first though." Carlos nodded in agreement. Before I could ask, he asked me the question.

"Hey, um so what's up with that new prisoner they brought in?"

"I don't know Carlos, he's an oddball prisoner. Maybe since you belong to one of these great prison gangs here, I am sure you'll find out everything there is to find out about him," I told him.

Carlos gave me a look and smirked; he told me that I was right about that. But that his people had tried finding out who this individual was but that no one knew anything. "Come on, that's preposterous," I said.

"Others have tried but everyone is tight-lipped about his identity," he replied, looking at me as he took one more last puff which finished the cigarette. At first, I just thought it was all poppycock that there was no such thing as not knowing anything. I firmly believe that someone had to know something. We as humans like to talk, so someone has to know something. Nothing ever stays hidden for long in this world. "Who knows, who he is or what he is," Carlos said.

"Oh my God, you Mexicans and your superstitions are the best." I chuckled.

"Hey, Silas, sometimes it's good to be superstitious. There is a lot in this world that we don't understand," Carlos said. I was trying to rationalize what Carlos was telling me, but my logical mind was not letting me process the superstitious part of our conversation. "Of course, if there is anything, we find out I will be sure to let you know first thing," Carlos told me as he left to join his group. Although I made a joke about Carlos' superstitious assumption, I couldn't help but think about the prisoners' peculiarities.

When everyone was back in their cells, Jeremy Brown was shouting obscenities to the weird prisoner whose cell was right across from his. "What are you in here for?" Brown asked. But he got no reply. "Hey, I am talking to you mother fucker!" Brown said to him again, now his tone of voice was more agitated. But still there was utter silence on his end.

"Leave him alone. Stop badgering him with questions that are of no concern to you," Carlos shouted from his adjacent cell to Brown.

"Shut the fuck up before I make you my bitch Carlos, like I did when you first showed up here. Do you remember?" Brown recalled.

"Fuck you," Carlos responded. Brown began making lewd comments and movements, basking in his recollection of his sexual encounter with Carlos.

"Stop it. It's not a proud thing you should be relieving Brown, we all go through shit like that as you did when you came here as well," I responded.

"Fuck you, Silas," he shouted from his cell.

"How many times did I have to save you?" I asked. "Until one day I did not arrive on time," I reminded him.

However, Brown was stuck in his ways that he kept on pushing that man's buttons. Until he got a reaction out of him, and it was terrifying. We all witnessed that spectacle about what happened to Brown. Sometimes, when I close my eyes, I relive everything. Most people I've written to I've told them about what I witnessed and they either think

I am full of shit, or they think that I should be used to things like that since I am in prison. They don't seem to grasp the difference between man doing harm to others and when it is a supernatural element. Well, it was lights out. And so Brown continued muttering things to the mysterious man. "I told him to keep his comments to himself, that we all were trying to sleep." But he just scoffed at my remark, and he never once relented.

He was so focused and headstrong about saying rude, and sexual remarks to this man it was beyond me. Well, all we heard was, "Oh so you finally decided to get up off your ass and spit shit back at me!" Brown shouted. That's when we first heard him speak, part of me was curious to hear what he sounded like and another part of me wished I'd never heard him speak.

"You're a feeble man, Brown, if you wish to speak to me in a more etiquette way, I suggest you start trying harder," he responded. His voice was deep but somewhat guttural.

"What the fuck. What the hell do you mean?" Brown asked in an angry tone of voice.

"I think he's insulting your intelligence," Francis Jacobs replied, laughing.

"Mother fucker, this shit isn't going to fly with me, thinking you're smarter than me; if you haven't noticed where you are, let me tell you you're in my house because your decisions weren't always the brightest if you ended up here," Brown said.

"Haha, I chose to be here, that's the difference between you and I," he responded. He placed his giant hands against the bars and leaned forward.

"Hey, you can't bend those bars if that's what you're trying to do, it's impossible," Francis said to him in a stern voice. At this point, Carlos and I woke up from our bunks and we stuck our arms out holding up our mirrors to see if we could see him as the dense light of the moon illuminated our cell block. I could make out that he was so tall, and he was indeed leaning up against the bars as if he was trying to separate the bars in order to get out.

To be truthful, his musculature scared me and actually terrified me. No man could ever get that big as the body would give out. "What the hell," I heard Carlos whisper.

"Shhh," I said to Carlos. Brown on the other hand put on a brave face and continued dissing him shouting cuss words at him. Trying to make him feel less of a man. He pulled out every stop everything his feeble mind could come up with.

"Stop, Brown, you see I am already getting bored and when I get bored well that's when the fun begins," he replied. As he pushed himself against the bars again. He made it seem as if he was doing pushups. I felt something hit my head. When I looked up, I saw the roof slowly begin to crack.

"Ay, Brown I think you should cool it, I think that's what he wants you to do, he wants you to tell him things because I don't think he's human," I told Brown. And, as soon I said that he wasn't human I saw through my mirror his eyes as he made a quick head movement and glanced over at me. His eyes were red, and his pupil was super dilated and pitch black. Both Carlos's mirror and mine shattered in our hands, cutting our hands. "Ahh," we both yelled in pain.

Having witnessed all that I thought that would've done it for Brown, but it didn't. It only pissed him off more. It's as if he was under its spell. A spell of some kind. He continued and continued until all of a sudden there was some wheezing noises, you know the type you make when you can't breathe. Along with some gurgling noises as well. So we started yelling for the guards but as always, the guards were taking their sweet time, or ignoring us as they've done in the past. An inmate was being killed by something otherworldly and they didn't care. As Brown laid there on the floor of his cell wheezing and gurgling, we all heard what appeared to sound like bones or body parts contorting. It is truly an awful sound to make and hear.

I saw Francis in complete awe as he was witnessing everything. His cell was next to Brown's and across from this thing's cell. Carlos and I motioned him to tell us what he was seeing, and he mouthed us the words, "He just passed through the fucking bars, his body contorted, what the fuck." Suddenly, I heard Carlos begin to pray and I told him to shut up before that thing set his sights on him next. Thankfully, he listened to me and quieted himself. We saw him walk up to Brown's cell with a quick movement of the hand. The cell door that was securely fastened, opened up as if he had used some kind of magic trick. He walked right in and picked up Brown off the floor without touching him. It's as if he was doing it with his mind or something. I really can't explain it. He slammed him against the walls and then he lifted him super high and dropped him on the floor. He did that for several minutes until he got bored. That's when he decided to just cram his body into the cell bars just like that. After he did that the cell door opened and he contorted his body to get back into his cell and headed to sleep.

Carlos, Francis, and I just stood there in shock. We didn't know what to say. Our minds couldn't process what we had just witnessed. The following morning Louie and Bradley came into the cell block. They headed straight to Brown's cell as if they knew what had gone down last night. As they stood there shocked, standing in front of Brown's cell, "What in the world happened here?" they asked. Fearing for our lives we all said that we didn't know what had happened to Brown. They both scratched their heads in bewilderment. They turned around and questioned him. "Do you know what happened here?" they asked. To which he just shook his head. They seemed to be satisfied with his answer and they told us that the warden will follow up with us. After this brief conversation they left. Later that day they came for Brown's body and his death was ruled as a suicide from what I heard from Louie. No one ever mentioned Brown again. "Thanks, for not ratting me out," he told us from his cell.

We all stood there just in utter and complete shock. We didn't know how to process what we had just witnessed. It was appalling to me. "What was he?" I questioned. I pondered that question the rest of the day. When it was chow time, I was sitting down by myself at the spot where I usually ate, when suddenly I heard the slamming of a metal tray. I looked up and to my shock it was him. He smirked and asked if he could join me. By this time word got out about what had happened with Brown and every inmate respected this individual. Moreover, I think they were scared of him. Even the worst of the worst inmates were intimidated by him. I nodded and motioned him to sit down, while the rest of the inmates looked at me wondering what my move was going to be. I knew deep down some wanted me to do something stupid by challenging this person so I could end up dead. But I however knew better, and so I didn't give them the satisfaction that they all so much wanted to see. Once, they saw that I had been respectful and very collected. They turned around and went about the rest of their pitiful lives. "Silas, correct?" he asked, preparing himself to eat.

"Yes that's correct and you are?" I asked him. Now as he sat across from me, I could see every detail of his skin, every scar on his face. He was completely covered in scars but I was sure every scar told a story. He never once lifted his head to address me even when he asked to sit. His head was down. But I could clearly see how disheveled he looked. And somehow his voice was different than the one that had answered Brown. His voice was that of a human. Pfft he even looked humanoid to me. I knew what I had witnessed the night of Brown's demise, but my mind however couldn't or wouldn't comprehend how that could be. A mental illness perhaps I thought to myself. My mind was still trying to process everything and be logical about the whole situation when I heard him telling his name.

"Ciel, that's my name," he responded.

"Ciel." I told him that's a unique name. "Where's it from?" I asked.

"It doesn't matter," he responded. Fearing retaliation from his part I decided not to press the matter any further.

"Ahem," I said as I continued to eat my food and break the utter silence between us. "What are you in for?" I dared to ask. But I followed it up with, "If you wish to tell me though, if you don't feel right then it's all right, I completely understand." Which was a complete lie because deep down my curiosity was getting the best of me. I really wanted to know who this person was. What he was in there for. In the back of my mind I frequently thought that maybe Mateo had somehow found a way to get even with me for taking out his friends. That maybe he had sent this degenerate after me and that one of these days I would end up dead. Although I didn't care either way, still I needed to know about this man everything I could possibly know. In that particular moment that we were eating for the first time, he looked up at me. He smiled through the side and said, "I am in here on the same charge as you."

"What do you mean by the same charge as me?" I asked.

"We don't have to be coy with each other Silas, I know you're in here for double murder," he told me. His eyes were blue but with a purplish hue to them.

By this time "chow time" was over and we all returned to our cells. Although nothing fruitful came out of our little talk at "chow time" I knew that there would be other times. I thought to myself as I browsed through a magazine that I would maybe have to become more of a friend to him. Maybe then will he open up to me more. Maybe if he heard my story as to why I did, what I did, he wouldn't think that I was this coldhearted killer. I continued looking through the magazine and told myself that maybe he had seen something in me because he had decided to approach me out of everyone in the prison. But, deep inside of me, I tried to remain optimistic about this whole ordeal. I knew that he was not human. An ominous thought came over me as I thought that this nonhuman thing was literally next to me. What if one night he would go berserk and kill everyone at the prison. I was on high alert and my peace was gone once more, after I had that epiphany.

A few days later, I saw him in the yard. He was sitting across me so, I headed over to him. As I approached, I saw him looking straight at me. His eyes were cold and deadless. There was not a shred of human in this man or whatever he was. I sat down next to him, and I asked, "Who'd you kill?"

He turned around to look at me and replied, "A lot of people."

"Hmm," I responded. "Tell me Ciel, did they deserve to die?" I asked.

"Everyone deserves to die, it's just how someone dies that makes people remember them for years," he replied. He looked up at me and gave me a grin. He spoke in riddles sometimes or in terms you couldn't really comprehend and that bothered me a lot.

I was about to ask him a follow up question when I saw Carlos and Francis heading towards us. Judging by their worried expressions written on their faces, I could tell this wasn't good.

"We just came from speaking to the Warden," Carlos told us.

"What does he want?" I asked. Francis explained to Ciel and I that Brown's family didn't believe the story; the Warden had conjured up about it being a suicide. Francis continued explaining that the Family of the dead inmate had brought in the FBI to thoroughly examine the prison. The FBI said they would perform an investigation about this eerie death. "So what does that have to do with us?" I said.

"Well, they are going to interrogate each and every inmate within the cell block to see what initially happened," Francis said.

"Let's just hope that if others get questioned, they don't say nothing, because I really doubt that they didn't hear shit," Carlos responded. The three of us looked at Ciel waiting for a reply from him but all he said with his head down was, "Don't worry I'll take care of it." He got up and headed to go, see the Warden.

"Hey, um Silas, what do you think he's going to do to the Warden?" Carlos asked. I told Carlos I didn't know but that I hoped that no harm would come to the Warden.

"Any luck in trying to find out who he is?" Francis asked me. I shook my head , and told them that every time I tried asking him questions, he'd always respond with a riddle or an answer that made no sense. His answers are perplexing and enigmatic. Carlos and Francis looked at me, they too just as myself were dumbfounded. I mean the fact that no one knows who he is, just makes me question humanity's logic.

"Yes. Not to mention the fact that this guy contorted his body through the cell bars is so baffling," Carlos replied. We all just sat around debating what he could be or why he's even here. As Carlos and Francis expressed their own theories amongst themselves, I for one thought about him and how he quickly reacted the moment that the guys said the FBI had been brought in. The other two numskulls might've not noticed it, but I sure did. Once he heard this his body language changed. He stiffened up and became more reclusive. I put my hand on my chin and thought long and hard. "Why did he go and see the Warden?" "Why did his body language change when hearing about the FBI?" So many inquiries and yet so little answers, I thought to myself.

A few hours passed and we saw him heading over to us. "Do you think he told the Warden anything?" Francis asked. Both Carlos and I shook our heads in disagreement. He was heading straight to us when he was cut off by two of the prison gangs' Fiercest leaders. A man known as Marcos Guevarra and Dalton Pierce. "What's this fool doing?" Carlos whispered. We looked on as both leaders confronted the prisoner. They began getting hostile towards him. On realization, he was surrounded by members of both gangs. Now obviously myself along with the other two knew that he could easily kill all of them, but we decided to start heading that way to see if we could smooth things over. After all, if the FBI was going to start investigations, I don't think the Warden would want to see more ludicrous deaths piling up in his prison. Well, at least we didn't.

We arrived before the gang members tried anything. "What do you think you're doing?" Francis asked.

"Stay out of this, he needs to get what is coming to him," Dalton said.

"What are you talking about, Dalton?" Francis replied. Carlos and I were on high alert making sure that no one tried anything.

"Come on Ciel, don't listen to these assholes," I said grabbing him by the arm.

"I wouldn't do that," one of the gang members told me, giving me a dirty look.

"Look, you guys don't understand who you're up against here," Carlos told them. We explained to them that he could actually kill all of them and he wouldn't hesitate to do it. Marcos looked at us and scoffed. He said that he along with his gang weren't afraid of this pathetic man. He told us that he could have him eliminated by tomorrow if he chose to.

"He's just a man," he responded. Dalton then cut off Marcos by saying that he deserved to die because of that little stunt he pulled with Jeremy the FBI got called in. The three of us stayed looking at them because they didn't know what had happened that night. Marcos approached Carlos and told him that he was out of the gang and practically sentenced him to death. He threatened him saying that it didn't end well for traitors and that he better watch his back. Even though Carlos tried to remain calm and put on his big boy pants I could see he was scared.

We headed over to where we were sitting down before, and I could see Ciel giving a dirty look to Dalton and Marcos. I could tell that he was still infuriated by the whole encounter. "What did you tell the Warden?" Francis asked. Ciel looked up at Francis and said that he had told the Warden along with Louie and Bradley and the rest of the guards that he would take care of the agents that would be investigating the prison. "What makes you so sure you'd be able to protect us, or them for that matter," Francis replied.

"Look, all I want to do is live out the rest of my sentence in peace," he told Francis. Now at this point Carlos and I felt some hostility coming from Ciel towards Francis.

"I think you should back off Francis, let him do what he said he was going to do," Carlos told Francis who by this time was as agitated and as angry as Ciel was.

"We wouldn't be in this mess if he wouldn't have killed Jeremy," he told Carlos, shoving him in the process. I could feel the tension between the parties building up that I tried my best to keep a level head.

"Look right now we are all being fueled by anger and frustration, maybe even fear. I suggest you back off for the time being and let him deal with it," I suggested. Francis gave me a cold look and shook his head. He left the group and that was the last time we saw him alive. He was killed by one of his fellow gang members, the following day while lifting weights. He was stabbed multiple times. He died of his wounds a few hours later.

Following his death, I couldn't bear the thought that his last moments were spent arguing with Ciel, Carlos, and I.

"What made him turn on Ciel the way that he did?" I asked myself. Again my logical mind was trying to make sense of it all. "Hmm," I thought. I was beginning to come up with my own conclusion. When I heard chaos coming from Ciel's cell. This time we didn't have Francis to give us a heads up. But judging by the sound it sounded as if Dalton and Marcos had somehow found their way into Ciel's cell. "Hey!" I shouted. As we heard the gushing of flesh being slashed opened as both men stabbed Ciel. We could hear groaning in agonizing pain as we continued to hear the way his flesh was being slashed. Both men laughed maniacally as if they enjoyed what they were doing to him. Blinded by their own rage and fuel to kill, they went to town on Ciel, stabbing, kicking, punching him. 'All the fun stuff' as Dalton would say. If you ask me, Dalton was a piece of human garbage and he deserved everything that would be coming to him, so was Marcos. Both men made me sick to my stomach.

After a while of us yelling and shouting Louie and

Bradley came rushing in. They were able to control the situation. They took Dalton and Marcos and placed them in solitary confinement far away from us. As they led them out of our cell block both men were drenched in Ciel's blood, and they both cackled as they passed by our cells. "Son of a bitch," I heard Carlos tell Marcos.

"You're next, bitch," Marcos replied to Carlos as he spat on him.

"Go to hell, asshole," Carlos replied.

"All right, that's enough Marcos lets go," Bradley told him.

"What about Ciel, is he going to be okay?" I asked in a concerned tone.

"We will come back and see if he needs any help," Louie shouted back. It was at this point that Carlos and I both realized that we considered this man a friend of ours. "If he is hurt badly, Silas, we need to protect him," Carlos told me from his Cell. I told him that I agreed with him in that sense. Later, Carlos and I watched in sheer sadness as Louie and Bradley brought the gurney into his cell and wheeled him out. He looked to be hurt badly. He was lying down on the gurney and as they wheeled him past our cells, he smiled at us a huge smile from ear to ear. The smile he gave us revealed a mouth of pointy teeth. The smile was not that of a don't worry I'll be okay kind of smile, no, this smile he gave us was more of a revenge type of smile. His eyes were black with red which we knew meant he was out for blood. Carlos and I stopped fretting when we realized he had set his sights on Dalton and Marcos and there was not a place in this whole prison they could hide that he wouldn't find them.

A month passed when that incident occurred and Ciel was still in the infirmary. "He was in bad shape, not so much now," the doctor said, redressing his wounds.

"Yes we can see that, when is he getting out of here though?" Carlos asked curiously. The Doctor said he couldn't really tell us. He said that he had suffered almost life-threatening injuries. He then procrastinated for a few minutes and told us in a low tone of voice. "However, I am a little perplexed about his injuries." Carlos and I pretended not to know where he was going with this. Well, he told us that while Ciel had sustained life-threatening injuries that it's like he was a fast healer and that his vitals appeared normal. We looked at him in disbelief and he said, "Look I took pictures of him when he was first brought in." He showed us the picture and he had more wounds than he had now. The ones the doctor redressed were the ones that were still visible. "What the hell is he?" the Doctor asked.

"We ask ourselves the same question, but we have yet to find an answer." The Doctor looked at both of us and then looked at him and left the room.

All of sudden we heard, "Is he gone?" We turned around and since our backs were to him.

And Carlos gave a huge smile and said, "Ay, Ciel, we thought you were gone!" he told him.

Ciel looked at him and said, "Nope I am still here."

I looked at him and said, "You and I both know you could've taken those guys out, why'd you hold back?" I asked. At first, he was silent but then he told us he held back because it wasn't yet time for him to end their lives with all these Federal agents coming into the prison and investigating, but their day is going to come and he will make sure that their deaths don't come quick enough. His eyes became red and his pupils dark. We saw his face become distorted with razor pointy sharp teeth that stretched from ear to ear. Carlos and I just stood there watching this man transform into this grotesque type of monster. However, we didn't care. This sense of calmness and safety overcame both of us. And that is when we made the decision that we had to protect this man at all costs.

In a few months Ciel was out of the infirmary and was back to our cell block. I was glad he was back, and Carlos was too. All of sudden the prison doors opened to our cell block and two FBI agents entered the prison. They wanted to remain inconspicuous but come on they weren't fooling anyone. They spoke to inmates and took down their accounts of what happened on the night in question. Some inmates gave credible recollections. Others however seemed reluctant to talk. I guess they didn't wish to get involved in this mess. Others were more than willing to disclose their hatred for Jeremy Brown saying that he got what he deserved. Finally, after speaking to Carlos they reached my cell as well. The prison guard opened my cell door and they both stepped inside. I was the only one that they spoke to inside the cell. They said that they felt that they didn't need to worry about me. They said I was considered low risk. "Can you tell us about what happened to Mr. Brown that night?" one of the agents asked. He introduced himself as Zachary Markle and the other agent introduced himself as Devin Rodriguez.

"I am pretty sure they've already told you what you wanted to know," I replied.

"Yes, we've heard a few things but we are conducting

a thorough investigation and so we have to make sure we get everyone's opinions on the matter," Agent Rodriguez said. He looked at me with displeasure in his gaze. Frankly, I wasn't too fond of his stare towards me. I had always been a confrontational man and so this stare provoked the inner beast within me that I had been suppressing for the longest time.

"Agent Rodriguez, I suggest that you stop looking at me that way or I won't oblige," I responded. Rodriguez broke the intimidating gaze almost immediately and hung his head.

"Agent Markle, Jeremy Brown committed suicide," I answered.

"What makes you so sure that he committed suicide?" Rodriguez asked. I smirked slightly and told them that I knew that Brown had been feeling depressed lately. I told them that Brown had a tendency to hurt himself. They looked at each other as if they couldn't grasp what I was telling them. "Ahem, while that might be true, if he did kill himself, it doesn't explain how his body was found," Markle replied. Both agents looked at me as if they knew that some oddity surrounded Jeremy Brown's death. Deep inside me I didn't know what they wanted me to say. Ciel had promised the warden that he would take care of these individuals, yet they were still here plaguing me with questions. I nodded in agreement with the agents. "It is odd that someone would commit suicide by cramming himself through the cell bars, don't you think Silas," Rodriguez asked.

"Well, people can surprise you sometimes by the way they kill themselves," I said. Even though I knew that my response didn't really sway their minds, I really hoped that they would just get out of here and get out of my space. Finally maybe they got the hint and they headed towards Ciel's cell. However, they didn't enter the cell, they just stood outside and asked him questions about what happened that night. Ciel was quick to answer their questions and so they could continue their investigation. After, they interrogated everyone at the prison and after long consideration they determined that his death was indeed a suicide. They closed the case and all matters ended just like that. Now I am not sure but the agent's curious natures seemed to change when they headed over to Ciel's. Even though they didn't interact with him personally, I felt like he swayed their minds somehow.

"Hmm," I thought to myself. "Could he have the ability to possess mind control over what is going on, the thought that weird coincidences are happening is just perplexing me leaving me baffled," I thought to myself. "Could it be that he was a weird experiment that went rogue after being contained in a laboratory?" I asked myself. I was trying to bring some logical sense to all this phenomenon going on around me. I placed my hand on my chin and paced around in my cell. By doing this it always made me think. "Maybe he's an alien sent here by his fellow comrades for some malicious intent over the human race?" I asked again. My mind could not compute what my thought process was trying to rationalize. But how could I not think he was some kind of other worldly being if he was far too weird.

"So Ciel, I want to thank you from the bottom of our hearts," the warden came rushing through the doors of the prison. Interrupting my process of thoughts.

"Yes, we are in debt to you we could've lost our jobs yet you saved us all," Louie replied with a smile. Ciel nodded and said that they were welcome, from that day forth a pact was made between the Warden and Ciel. Although, I admit I was a bit jealous I still felt that he deserved everything good that happened to him. After all Jeremy was being a jerk to him and he just wouldn't let up, and so he got what he deserved in the end. Once the Warden and the guards left, I pressed myself against the wall and asked him.

"So Ciel, what did you do to get them to leave and close the case?"

He looked at me and responded with, "Mind control, telepathy, that sort of thing." My jaw dropped. I just couldn't believe that there was such a thing. Never in my life did I think I would be witness to it.

"You have to teach me how to do that," I said with a huge grin on my face.

A few months passed and we were taken out to the yard for exercise. Ciel, Carlos, and I were just talking amongst ourselves when we saw Ciel becoming agitated. "What's wrong Ciel?" Carlos asked, looking concerned.

Ciel replied, "Look who's heading this way," tightening his teeth in rage.

"Ahi dios mio," Carlos replied, rolling his eyes in petty disgust.

"Don't worry Ciel, these sons of bitches won't do anything besides Carlos and I got your back," I reassured him.

"Of course, we got your back," Carlos confirmed. Now all three of us knew exactly why Dalton and Marcos were heading this way. This confrontation was taking place for three reasons. Reason one: was because all the drugs that were coming into the prison were being distributed by Ciel, Carlos, and I. We were knocking down their business. All the inmates preferred getting supplied by us because Ciel could literally astral project and travel to places to get the drugs. Hustling and meddling in their business was a huge no. Reason 2: was because they still had it in for Ciel and wanted him dead. Somehow they had found out that he was still alive. But both men were too proud to make allies with us. I thought that they would be more open to the idea of becoming friends. I mean it could've potentially saved their little prison drug smuggling business they had going on. And the final reason was because they were just bitter that Ciel was now the top person in the prison, and they couldn't have that. They didn't want to relinquish control to this thing as they called him. Now looking back, I really wished things could've ended differently for both men. Yet, both men were so vain and so mad with power that they couldn't just leave well enough alone.

"Hey, we know what you've been doing and that doesn't sit well with us!" Marcos yelled in a stern voice. Dalton nodded in agreement with Marcos.

"Look, what do you want?" I said looking at both men. Although both of them attempted to stare me down none of it worked.

"Stop acting coy with us, Silas, you know why we are here all three of you do," Dalton answered with a low deep voice that trembled in anger.

"Wow, we must've really pissed them off," I thought to myself. I smirked and said nonchalantly, "Hey you can't blame us if our stuff is better."

Dalton shoved me and said, "You think I am playing, asshole!" By this time, every inmate in the yard headed over to where the confrontation was taking place due to Dalton's loud voice.

"He wasn't trying to be funny, rather just telling it like it is, you both should just take your losses and get out of our faces before it is too late," Carlos replied, shoving Dalton back.

Dalton laughed sadistically and told Marcos, "You're boy, I suggest you handle him just like I handled mine for disrespecting me and turning his back on those that took care of him when no one else would've."

Marcos looked at us three up and down and said, "We will get you one by one you'll see, slowly we will lift our business back up. However, Dalton we do have one problem and that is this son of a bitch right here Ciel."

"I agree with you that he is part of the problem, I guess we will have to try harder to kill him," Dalton said. All of a sudden, a huge fight broke out between us and the two of them. Soon all their gang members started wailing at us too. But even though Carlos and I were getting the shit beat out of us by their minions, as we laid on the floor, we saw Ciel holding his own against Marcos and Dalton. I was beginning to see the transformation because of his anger that he had suppressed for so long. So I told Carlos he is transforming and his demon is coming out. Marcos and Dalton were so oblivious to witness what was going on because they were hellbent on inflicting pain unto him. All of a sudden, we heard a gushing sound and smashing of what sounded like fluid and squishy tissues of some sort.

Now what I witnessed was terrifying. I saw him smash Dalton and Marcos's heads open. He smashed them with tremendous force that brain matter splattered all over the place. All the inmates screamed as Ciel transformed into this diabolical entity. They all ran away terrified that they might be next as he just threw their lifeless bodies on the ground like they meant nothing. He then changed into his human form and picked us up even though our bodies had suffered a lot of damage. Every bone in our bodies hurt like hell. Our eyes were swollen shut and our mouths were completely swollen. "Are you guys okay? Are you guys in any pain?" he asked.

We both said a little bit but it's nothing that we both couldn't handle. He looked at us and raised an eyebrow.

"You seem skeptical," said Carlos. He just smiled and said it's typical for humans to be stubborn. I didn't dare to look at the remains of the discarded bodies. Soon Bryan and Louie showed up and assessed the carnage.

"Ciel, again," they said.

"I had to do what I had to do," he replied. They placed their hands on their hips and took off their hats and scratched their heads. I guess they were thinking of what to do with the bodies of those creeps. From that day forward after that little display of Ciel's influence it was smooth sailing for us along with the prisoners. Everyone was content and respected him. However, it wasn't until Ciel had this idea about busting out of here. He brought up the idea to us during chow time. "Are you serious, Ciel, how the hell are we supposed to get out of this place?" I asked. He looked at me with a blank stare.

He said, "I've been studying this place for a while now.

I know the surroundings super well. There is a weak part on the fence in the rear end of the prison. The chain link is weak so we can get out through there." Carlos and I looked at each other. What he was proposing was forbidden to do. If we were to get caught even attempting to flee, we could get more years added to our sentence.

"You both are in here for life so what's the risk of getting caught," he told us. "What do you have to lose?" he asked. To us it sounded more like he was taunting us. So Carlos agreed and so did I. He smiled a huge grin and said, "That's what I love to hear." Then we both proceeded to ask him where we would find refuge. No one would want to harbor fugitives. He smiled evilly again and told us not to worry, that he knew of a place where a lot of strange things are hidden and no one even knows about that place.

Carlos laughed and said, "You're joking right, I mean it's odd to think a place like that exists and no one knows about it." Ciel told us that it might sound so good to be true but that such a place did exist. He knew about it because that's where he came from. Both of us couldn't believe what we were hearing.

"Tell us more please, we are curious," I told him.

He smiled and said, "I knew you were curious about me the first time you all saw me. I am different from most around here." Carlos and I agreed with that statement. We continued to pressure him into telling us where it was like where he was from and why was here. He looked at us for a while before he went silent. Carlos and I looked at each other shocked. We didn't know what to say or think. Perhaps we had angered him because of our enthusiastic nature. Why he had stopped talking was absurd.

"Look, we just want to know what we are getting into Ciel that is all," Carlos said. Carlos' gaze was now staring at the floor. He continued to be silent and finally after a few minutes he spoke again.

"Even though you have proven that you two are trustworthy; I don't wish to disclose anything about where I come from. I find it best if you see it with your own eyes," he told us.

"So you're not even going to tell us about those scars you have?" I asked. By now my tone of voice was more assertive towards him. I couldn't help but feel betrayal on his part. For him to still conceal fundamental things such as his upbringing, what he had done spoke really ill about the kind of person he was.

Even though I thought all these things about him and his ability to hide crucial things I still felt the urge to follow him. As we headed back to our cells, I sent a note to Carlos in which I wrote: *Hey, Carlos are you scared?* To which he replied *Somewhat, but yet it's as if I gravitate towards him, the urge to follow this guy is so strong.* To which I replied that I had the same feelings and that I did find it odd. I later got a note from Ciel which read: *A new life awaits you both, we leave at midnight, pass it on to Carlos.* After receiving the note and Carlos reading it, he whispered to me, "How are we supposed to leave if we are in our prison cell?" he asked.

Ciel replied, "Just be ready by three a.m. I will handle the rest."

Well it was a dark and stormy night and thunder could be heard for miles. The thunder was so loud it's as if the whole planet was yelling in anger. The floor beneath my feet rumbled. I felt like I was going to get swallowed whole by the earth. I looked at my watch and it was exactly three a.m. All of a sudden, I heard Ciel chanting. When the lighting shone in through my cell window I saw his shadow. He appeared to be in front of a wall in his cell making some hand symbols. I saw as the lightning flashed again his long pointy fingernail cut through the prison wall. He got out of his cell and headed towards mine and then Carlos. Then in his demonic form he guided us out of there. Through the rumbles and the huge bad storm no one saw us leave. We ran through the prison yard and headed towards the weak part of the chain link fence. We got through without a problem and headed into the nearby woods.

We walked through the woods soaking wet and tired. We must've walked through the woods for hours. "How much further Ciel?" I asked.

"Not far. A few more miles," he said. Inside of me I wanted to pop off on him because I thought he had this all planned out but by the looks of it he didn't think this through. I wanted to tell him off because I was so frustrated. I was cold, wet and hungry. The fact that I hadn't eaten anything also didn't make me happy. We continued walking for a few more hours when he said, "Here is the getaway car." We were greeted by two beautiful women who seemed to know Ciel. One of them introduced herself as Sethe McGregor and the other one as Chrissy winters. We climbed aboard and they took us to our freedom. Finally as the sun rose Ciel smirked and said, "Boys I give you Crescent Falls." Carlos and I were mesmerized by the beauty of this place. It was a magical Oasis at least that's the vibe that I got from this place.

"Yes guys it is a magical place," he responded looking at us. It's as if we were meant to find this place. If you believe in the whole serendipity theory this is what it felt like. We got out of the car and just took in every bit of fresh air.

"They won't find you here no one does when you set foot into this town" Chrissy said.

"I am glad you're here Ciel. It took Mathius many years to find you but, when he did, well, everyone was stoked to have you around," Sethe told him.

Ciel grinned and said, "Well boys make yourselves at home and enjoy your freedom. And so months have passed and Carlos and I have become best friends. Our bond is stronger than ever. Ciel also has become a huge part of our lives. In the months that we've been in this town we came to learn so much. We came to learn that this town is run by five powerful families. With the last names of Winters, McGregor, McFlurry, Hall, and McMichaels. I've learned that this place harbors and protects individuals like us. People in this town are immortal, you could say. The reason Ciel couldn't speak about this town is that once you're in this town you can't speak to outsiders about it. Is this a curse? Or a blessing? I do not know, but a lot of people find themselves here when they do horrendous things. According to the men that run the town, every deity known to man, every magical entity is within the town's walls. Magic or sorcery as we all know is a sin and rejected by a lot of people. People who practice the art are condemned to hell by the church doctrine. I don't know what this place is. All I know is that I am happy to have found Ciel and Carlos is too. Maybe just maybe you, the reader will find your way to us soon if you dare to do something sinful, I am pretty sure that our paths will cross eventually.